Published in 2002 by Sterling Publishing Co., Inc.
387 Park Avenue South, New York, NY 10016

First published in Great Britain in 2001 by Brimax
an imprint of Octopus Publishing Group Ltd
2-4 Heron Quays, London E14 4JP
© 2001 Octopus Publishing Group Ltd

Library of Congress Cataloging-in-Publication Data Available

10 9 8 7 6 5 4 3 2 1

Distributed in Canada by Sterling Publishing Co., Inc.
C/o Canadian Manda Group, One Atlantic Avenue, Suite 105
Toronto, Ontario, Canada M6K 3E7

Sterling ISBN 0-8069-7835-X

OG THE DOG AND THE UNINVENTOR

WRITTEN BY
ANDREW MURRAY

Sterling Publishing Co., Inc.
New York

ILLUSTRATED BY
TERI GOWER

Jack was racing on his bike. And Og, his dog,
was trying to keep up with him.
It was a perfect day.
"I love the wind in my face!" said Jack.
"I love the colors of everything on a day like this!"

"But most of all, Og,
I love having you here to play with!"

"Woof!" said Og, who completely agreed.

... and she uninvented the wheel!

Crash!

Jack laid in a heap, tangled up in the bike frame.
There were no wheels on the bike anymore.
There were no wheels on anything!

Thanks to her, the Uninventor, the world was full of wheel-less bikes, wheel-less cars, wheel-less trains, and wheel-less skateboards.

Nobody could even remember what wheels were for!

The Uninventor did it again.
She uninvented rain!

And nobody could remember
what umbrellas were for!

"Woof!" said Og, who missed playing in the rain.

And then, she even uninvented ink!
And nobody could figure out
what pens were for!

What's this
plastic tube for?

She uninvented bolts, so ladders fell apart.
She uninvented writing, so books did not make sense.

She uninvented wind. The air felt very stuffy, but nobody knew why.

"Phew!" said Jack. "There used to be something that cooled us off on hot days. Where did it go?"

It wasn't just Jack.
People were puzzled. People were worried.
The world seemed to be missing so many things.
Nobody could remember exactly what was missing, but the world was definitely less interesting than it used to be.

She uninvented toothpaste.

So what were toothbrushes for?

She uninvented paint.

So what were paintbrushes for?

She uninvented money.

So wallets and piggy-banks were full of nothing.

She uninvented fur.

Kind people had to knit sweaters for
all the animals to keep them warm.

Jack knit one for Og.

All the things that made no sense were put in a museum.

The Museum of Thingless Things.

People went to the museum to stare and scratched their heads.

Until, that is, the Uninventor uninvented...

... museums!

She uninvented music, then uninvented sound.
She uninvented corners. Nothing looked the same!

She uninvented hairstyles, then uninvented hair.
How could she do this? What was she thinking?

She uninvented color, so a rainbow was seven shades of gray.
And oranges were gray. And Jack was gray. And Og was gray.

And *then... then... then...* she uninvented...

Og!

Jack could live with being...
hairless...
moneyless...
colorless...
but
being Og-less was something totally different!

Jack went to find out who did this.
He searched... and searched... and searched.

He followed the grayness...

he followed the emptiness...

and in the end, Jack found...

... the

Uninventor

The thoughtless,
careless,
friendless,
hairless,
Uninventor!

There was no sound for Jack to shout how he felt.
There was no writing for Jack to write how he felt.
There was no color for Jack to draw how he felt.

But he could still feel, and he felt... **ANGRY!**

The Uninventor felt Jack's feelings.
She looked around.

What a gray world! she thought.
What a dull, sad, silent, and empty world!

What have I done?
How can I put it right?

The Uninventor took a deep breath and...

POP!

She uninvented herself. She was no more.

And all the things she did were undone.
All the things she uninvented were
un-uninvented.

Jack liked the world how it was when
everything he loved was all around him...

... especially Og.